Dear Parent:

Congratulations! Your child is taking the first steps on an exciting journey. The destination? Independent reading!

STEP INTO READING® will help your child get there. The program offers five steps to reading success. Each step includes fun stories and colorful art. There are also Step into Reading Sticker Books, Step into Reading Math Readers, Step into Reading Phonics Readers, Step into Reading Write-In Readers, and Step into Reading Phonics Boxed Sets—a complete literacy program with something for every child.

Learning to Read, Step by Step!

Ready to Read Preschool–Kindergarten
• big type and easy words • rhyme and rhythm • picture clues
For children who know the alphabet and are eager to begin reading.

Reading with Help Preschool–Grade 1
• basic vocabulary • short sentences • simple stories
For children who recognize familiar words and sound out new words with help.

Reading on Your Own Grades 1–3
• engaging characters • easy-to-follow plots • popular topics
For children who are ready to read on their own.

Reading Paragraphs Grades 2–3
• challenging vocabulary • short paragraphs • exciting stories
For newly independent readers who read simple sentences with confidence.

Ready for Chapters Grades 2–4
• chapters • longer paragraphs • full-color art
For children who want to take the plunge into chapter books but still like colorful pictures.

STEP INTO READING® is designed to give every child a successful reading experience. The grade levels are only guides. Children can progress through the steps at their own speed, developing confidence in their reading, no matter what their grade.

Remember, a lifetime love of reading starts with a single step!

To Arden, the New Little Mayer

 Published in the United States by Random House Children's Books, a division of Random House, Inc., 1745 Broadway, New York, NY 10019, and in Canada by Random House of Canada Limited, Toronto. Originally published in different form as *Little Critter's Staying Overnight* by Golden Books, New York, in 1988, and subsequently published in adapted form in *Little Critter's Read-It-Yourself Storybook: Six Funny Easy-to-Read Stories* by Western Publishing Company, Racine, Wisconsin, in 1993. This 2011 edition was originally published by Golden Books, an imprint of Random House Children's Books, a division of Random House, Inc., in 1999.

Visit us on the Web!
www.stepintoreading.com
www.randomhouse.com/kids

Educators and librarians, for a variety of teaching tools, visit us at
www.randomhouse.com/teachers

Library of Congress Cataloging-in-Publication Data
Mayer, Mercer.
Little Critter sleeps over / by Mercer Mayer.
p. cm. — (Step into reading. A step 2 book)
Summary: Little Critter goes to visit a friend where someone in funny clothes opens the door, the napkins are folded to look like hats, and the bedroom is very dark.
ISBN 978-0-307-26203-5 (trade) — ISBN 978-0-307-46203-9 (lib. bdg.)
[1. Sleepovers—Fiction.]
I. Title. II. Series: Step into reading. Step 2 book.
PZ7.M462 Lb 2003 [E]—dc21 97080729

Printed in the United States of America
22 21 20 19 18 17 16 15 14 13

STEP INTO READING®

LITTLE CRITTER® SLEEPS OVER

BY MERCER MAYER

Random House New York

I am going to sleep over
at my friend's house.

His house is big.

Someone in funny clothes
opens the door.
I see my friend.

I say good-bye
to Mom.

I say hello
to my friend's pool.

We splash.
We swim.
We paddle.
We float.

We hit the ball
over the net.

Sometimes we hit the ball
too hard.

We play hide and seek
for a long, long time.

Then we go inside.
My friend has all of the
Bozo Builder set.

He has a train
that can loop around
and go fast.

His bear is big—
bigger than my bear.

But his dog
is small.
His dog is named
Froo-Froo.

It is time for dinner.
The napkin looks
like a hat.
I put it
on my head.

After dinner
we watch TV.
My friend has a TV
in his room.

It is time for bed.

We turn out the light.
It is dark—
darker than my room.

I pretend that
I am at home.
I hug my bear.

The next day
we play with the hose.
Froo-Froo likes
the hose, too.

No, Froo-Froo!
Come back!

We run.

We dive.

We jump.

We climb.

Got you!

It is time to go home.

I call Mom.

I say good-bye
to my friend.

Thank you
for everything.

Sleepovers
are fun.
But home is best.